SOMETHING'S FISHY

Jean Gourounas

Hey, what are you doing?

shh!

Are you fishing?

Hey, what's going on here?

I think she's fishing.

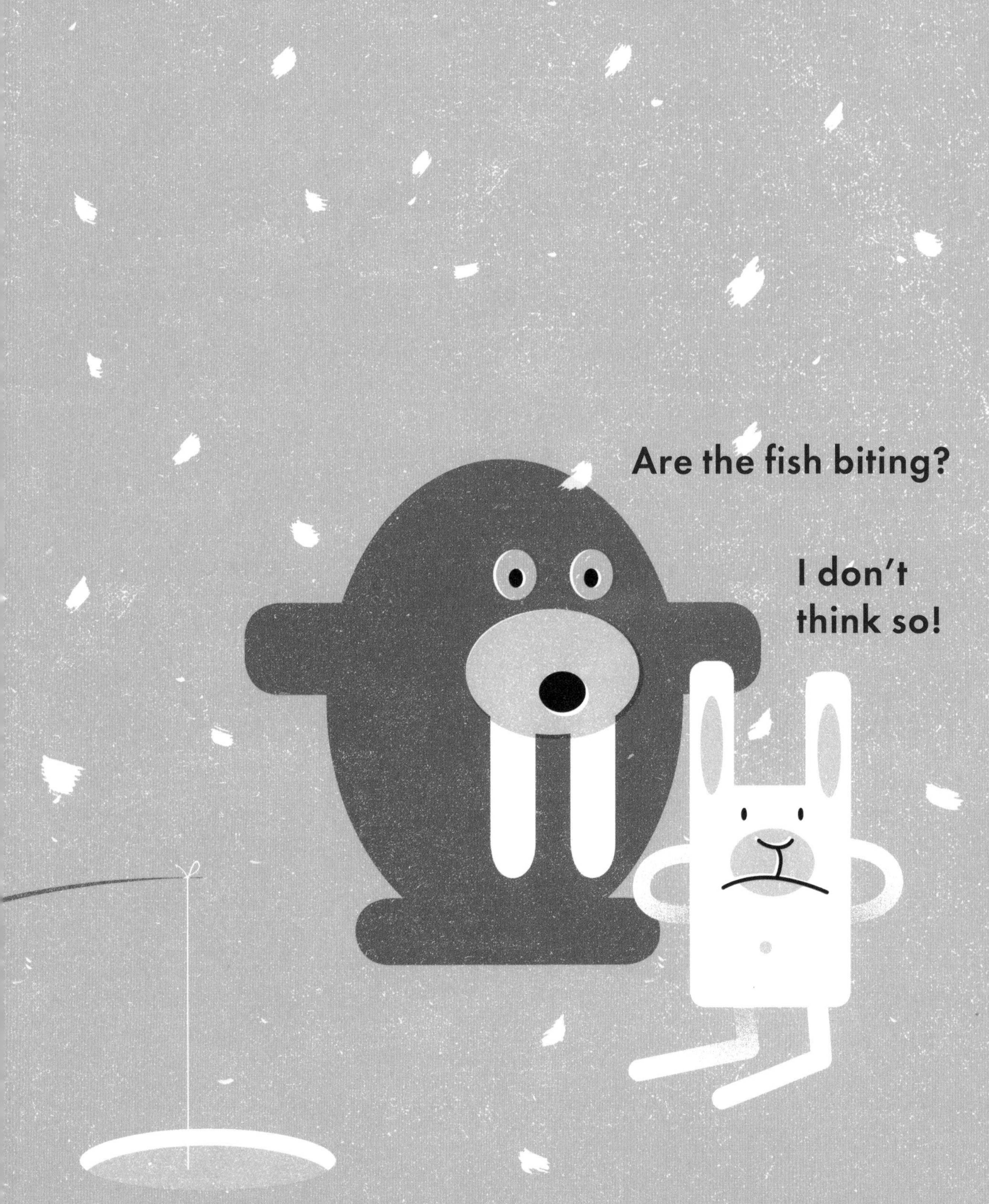
Are the fish biting?
I don't think so!

Hey, are you fishing?

Are any fish biting?

No!

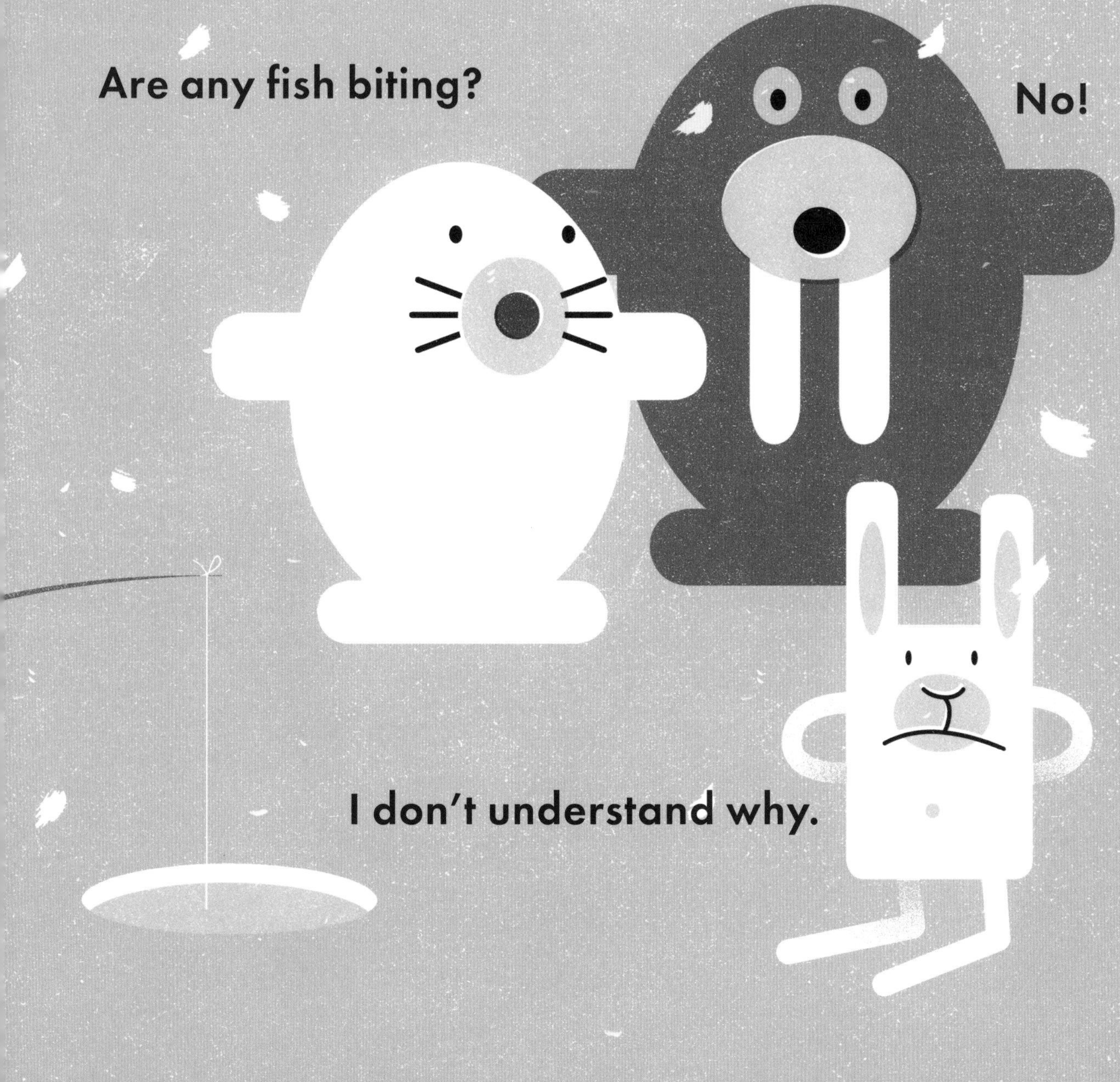

I don't understand why.

Is she fishing?

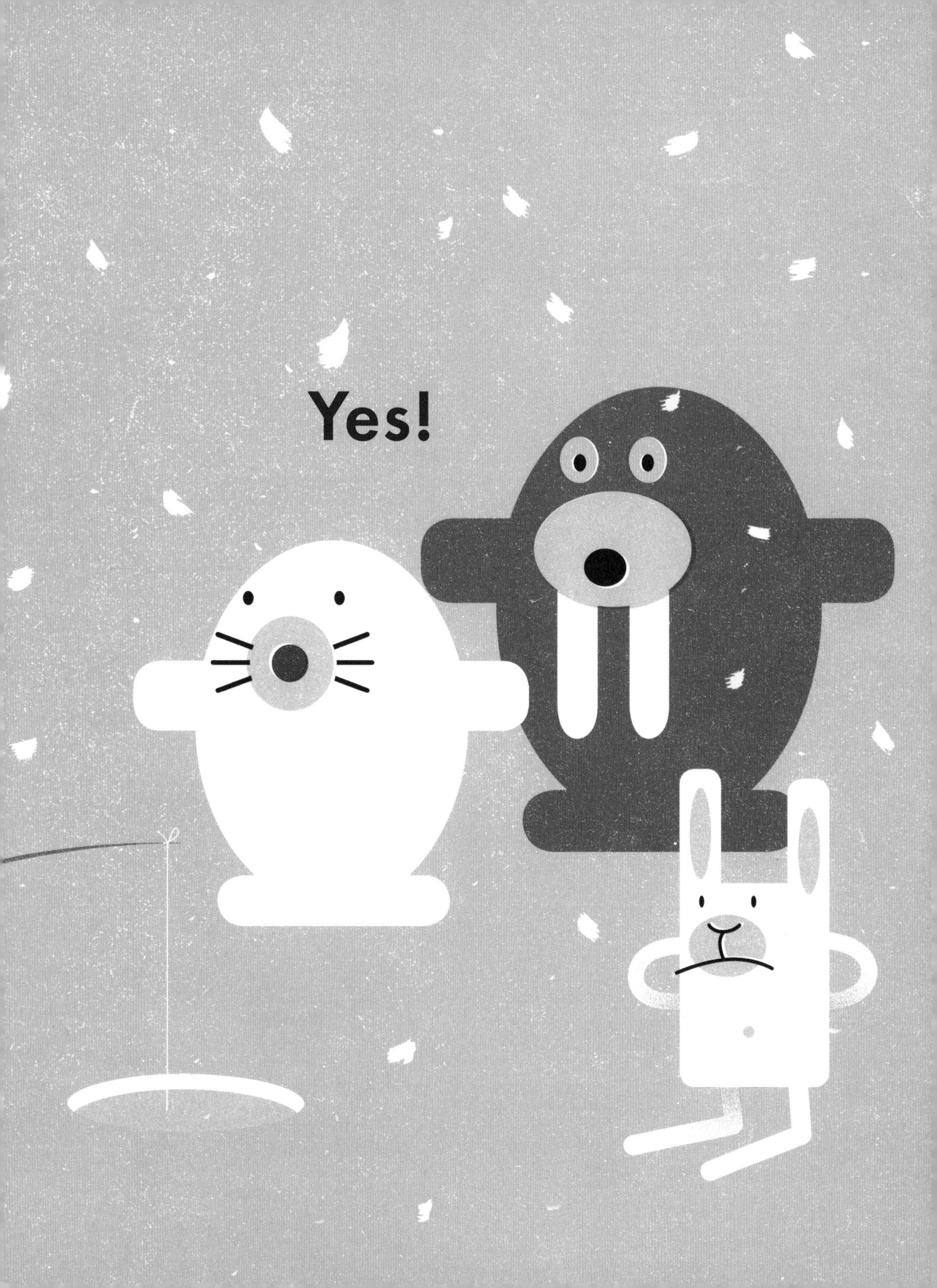
Yes!

So why aren't the fish biting?

We don't know!

I'm baffled.

Ooh, fishing!
Have you caught
anything?

No!

Why not?

We don't know!

I'm perplexed.

What's happening over here?

We're fishing!

But the fish
aren't biting!

Well, what did you put on the hook?

Some cake.

Cake? Who wouldn't
want a bite of cake?

I'm flummoxed.

There's cake
on the hook...

...but the fish
aren't biting!

Something's fishy!